D1469007

PLUMB MEMORIAL LIBRARY
7 CONSTITUTION WAY
ROCHESTER, MA 02770

BUZZ BOY AND FLY GUY

Tedd Arnold

Cartwheel
BOOKS®

SCHOLASTIC INC.
New York   Toronto   London   Auckland
Sydney   Mexico City   New Delhi   Hong Kong

For Marcus—stay inspired!
—T.A.

Copyright © 2010 by Tedd Arnold.

All rights reserved. Published by Scholastic Inc. SCHOLASTIC, CARTWHEEL BOOKS,
and associated logos are trademarks and/or registered trademarks of Scholastic Inc.

No part of this publication may be reproduced, stored in a retrieval system, or transmitted
in any form or by any means, electronic, mechanical, photocopying, recording, or otherwise,
without written permission of the publisher. For information regarding permission,
write to Scholastic Inc., Attention: Permissions Department, 557 Broadway, New York, NY 10012.

Library of Congress Cataloging-in-Publication Data
Arnold, Tedd.
Buzz Boy and Fly Guy / by Tedd Arnold.
p. cm.
Summary: Buzz creates a comic book that features Buzz Boy and Fly Guy as the superheroes.
ISBN 0-545-22274-5
[1. Flies--Fiction. 2. Cartoons and comics--Fiction. 3. Superheroes--Fiction.] I. Title.
PZ7.A7379Bu 2010 [E]--dc22
2009038925

ISBN 978-0-545-22274-7

10 9 8 7 6   11 12 13 14

Printed in Singapore   46
First printing, September 2010

A boy had a pet fly
named Fly Guy.
Fly Guy could say
the boy's name—

BUZZ!

One night Buzz said,
"I made a book.
We are the superheroes."

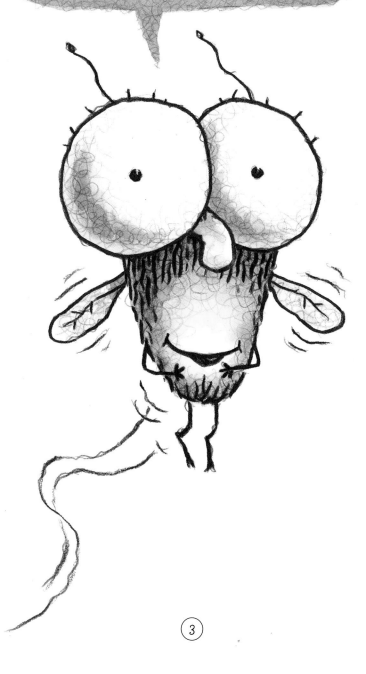

"Yes," said Buzz.

"I'll read it to you."

THE AMAZING ADVENTURES OF BUZZ BOY AND FLY GUY

BY ME (BUZZ)

CHAPTER ONE

ONE DAY BUZZ BOY WOKE UP.

YAWN

HE WAS THE SAME SIZE AS FLY GUY!

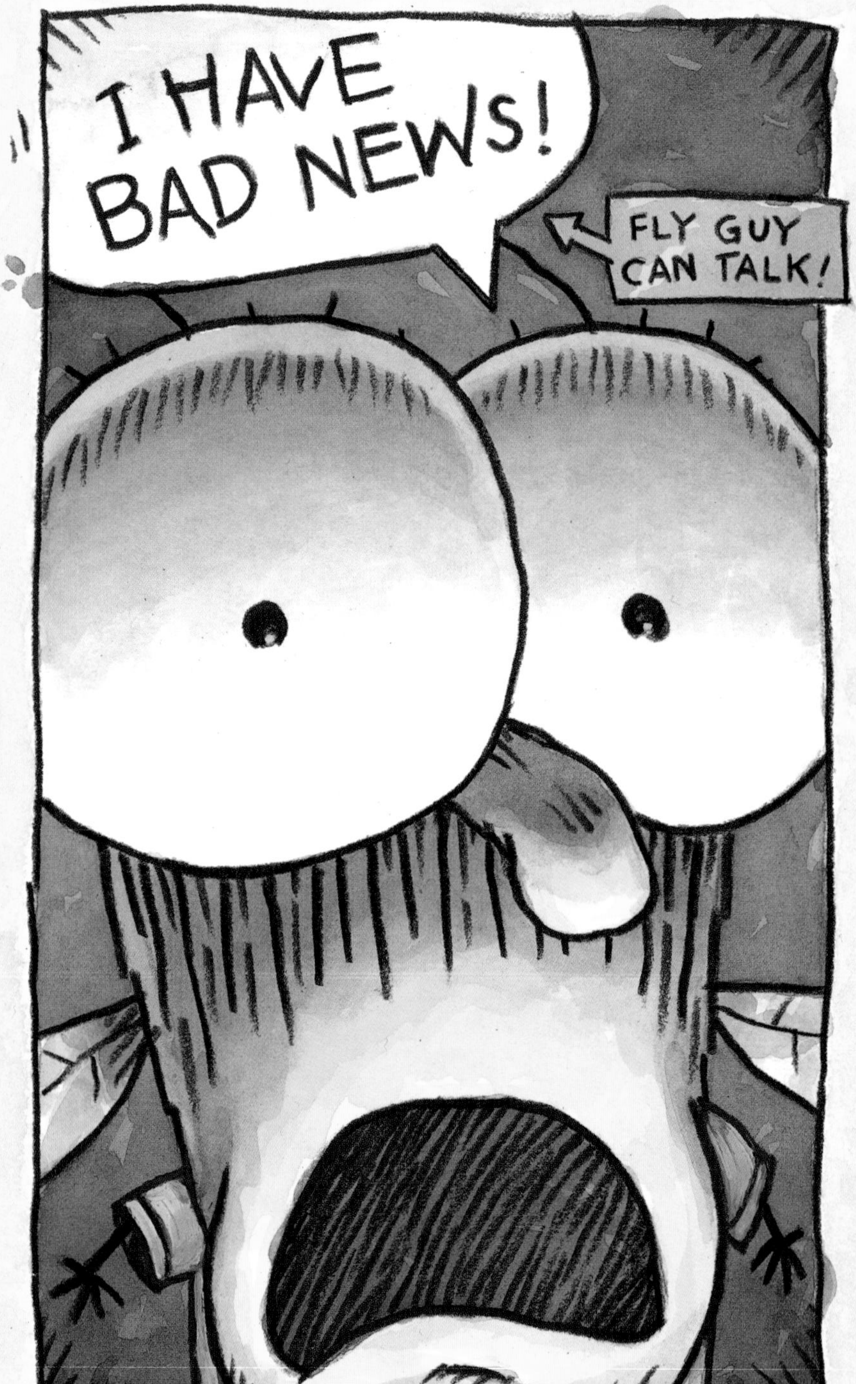
I HAVE BAD NEWS!
FLY GUY CAN TALK!

BUZZ BOY LOOKED OUT THE WINDOW.

HE SAW A SLEEPING DRAGON.

CHAPTER TWO

THE DRAGON WAS STILL ASLEEP.

WITH HIS SUPERSTRENGTH BUZZ BOY TURNED THE DRAGON AROUND.

FLY GUY USED HIS SUPERLOUDNESS.

THE DRAGON WOKE UP AND SHOT FIRE OUTSIDE.

CHAPTER THREE

BUZZ BOY AND FLY GUY
WERE PUT IN JAIL ON
THE PIRATE SHIP.

BUZZ BOY AND FLY GUY FLEW BACK TO THE ISLAND.

THEY MADE FRIENDS WITH THE DRAGON.

"The end," said Buzz.
Fly Guy said,

"Superheroes," said Buzz.
"Want to read it again?"

JUL -- 2012